"DOGNAPPED"

A SAFFY THE COCKAPOO STORY

BY

KEITH FLEMING

OTHER BOOKS BY THIS AUTHOR

(FOR CHILDREN AND DOG LOVERS)

The Adventures of Saffy the Cockapoo

More Adventures of Saffy the Cockapoo

(ADULT BOOKS)

The Twelfth of September

Quob House

The Ditcher

The Island Ray

Drakes Traitor

The Ring of Vice

Crimes of the Riverbank

All available on Amazon Books / Kindle

Life is settling down to a new routine for Saffy the Cockapoo, since the arrival of baby Katy in the Dobson household. It is a sort of humdrum existence for Saffy until the day she is 'dognapped'. Then everything changes.

This novel is a work of fiction and any resemblance to actual persons living or dead, is entirely coincidental.

CHAPTER 1.

Hello everyone, it's Saffy Dobson here again. You know, the cream coloured cockapoo who lives in deepest Dorset. Before I tell you my latest story, I think I had better update you all on the happenings within the Dobson household.

Mr and Mrs Dobson, that is Hubert and Eliza, had a baby girl last year and she is called Katy. Things were rather fraught for a while because Katy kept waking everyone up in the night and telling everyone she was hungry. Poor old Mr Dobson used to go off to work in the mornings looking as though he had hardly slept a wink all night and Mrs Dobson seemed at her wits end and also looked rather tired.

As for me, I tried to make the best of it and when Katy started crying, I tried to cover my head with my blanket and snuggle down deeper in my bed in the kitchen. Even so, my beauty sleep was disturbed, and I didn't feel quite myself when I woke up in the morning.

Mrs Dobson seemed so preoccupied with Katy that I think she forgot all about me from time to time. I used to get my food dished up at regular times, but now it arrived whenever Mrs Dobson remembered I needed feeding.

There was no doubt about it, Katy ruled the roost in the Dobson household, and everything revolved around her. It was not her fault; it was just a case that she needed looking after.

I used to be taken on long walks, sometimes with my best pal, Larry. He is the black Labrador who lives with Mr and Mrs Lawson in the corner house on our road. Us dogs were quite often let off the lead when we walked through the woods and onto the heath beyond, but we had to stay in earshot of the humans in case we had to be called back.

Unfortunately, since Katy arrived, Mrs Dobson seemed to be too busy to take me for long walks and I was lucky if I got a short walk around the houses. Sometimes Mrs Lawson would call round with Larry, and then she would offer to take me with them for a walk.

I really looked forward to those days when I could go out with Larry, and we would have a good gossip as we walked around, and I caught up with the local news.

Sometimes, when the children were not at school, I was allowed to call next door and play with the Rainey children. Roger their son liked to play ball and other games with me, but Joanna their daughter who had to use a special wheelchair just liked to watch me play and give me a cuddle.

Other than that, I felt as if I was not getting enough exercise and I had to wait until the weekend when Mr Dobson was home from work. Even then he did not get up very early and by the time he had washed and dressed and had his breakfast, it was almost lunch time before we went for a walk.

Things were never quite the same now that Katy had arrived and, in many respects, I felt left out. Occasionally in the evenings once Katy had gone to bed and Mr and Mrs Dobson collapsed onto the settee, I was allowed to join them, and Mrs Dobson would give me a cuddle just to let me know I had not been forgotten.

Life seemed to settle down into a sort of humdrum existence and as the months went by, Katy managed to go through the whole night without screaming to be fed. Mr and Mrs Dobson gradually lost that sort of frazzled look and things began to look up.

In the summer months, Katy was taken outside and allowed to roll around on a blanket on the lawn. I would lie down beside her, and she would giggle and reach out with her little hand. Sometimes she managed to grab a handful of my fur and pulled me, and I had to be rescued by Mrs Dobson from her clutches.

If Larry came on these occasions, both us dogs were allowed to play with Katy, but I was the only one who got their fur pulled, because Larry's coat was so much smoother than mine.

Then came the day when Katy learned how to crawl. Mr and Mrs Dobson were thrilled, but it was not so good for me as I had to keep a good lookout or else my fur would be pulled if Katy managed to make it to where I was lying.

One day, things took a turn far more serious than having my fur pulled. Katy was getting quite mobile and would crawl around quite fast, especially in the kitchen where there was linoleum laid on the floor.

I had been having a snooze in my basket in the kitchen and I heard Mrs Dobson come in with Katy. She put Katy on the floor whilst she got my food ready, but Katy just sat in the corner not taking any notice of anything. I was vaguely aware of Mrs Dobson putting my bowls of food on the floor, alongside my bowl of water.

I watched her do it through half closed eyes and thought I would have a little longer with my snooze before I went to eat. As Mrs Dobson turned to the sink to wash some things up, Katy went into action. Like greased lightening she began to crawl and made a beeline for my food bowls.

I was now fully awake and sat up with concern as she reached the bowls and stuck her hand into one of them. She picked up some of my food and put it in her mouth. I was amazed. She had her own food to eat, but now she was coming to eat mine as well.

I don't think she quite enjoyed the food as much as I would have done, because most of it went down her front and made a mess of her clothes. Then with a little laugh, she made for the other bowl containing my biscuits and picked up a handful, dropping several biscuits in the process. The dropped biscuits made a noise as they fell back into the bowl and Mrs Dobson turned round to see what was happening.

With a cry of alarm, Mrs Dobson quickly bent down and stopped Katy eating my biscuits, for which I was truly grateful, but when she saw the mess Katy had made trying to eat my meat, she got quite cross. Katy was picked up and plonked on the draining board and Mrs Dobson had to wash her face and then tried to get the mess off her clothes.

"I'm sorry, Saffy," said Mrs Dobson. "I'll get you some more food later, but first I'm going to have to sort Miss Dobson out and change her clothes."

I woofed to let her know I understood and as soon as they had left the kitchen, I ran straight to my bowls and ate my food quick before Katy came back for a second go.

A little later, Mrs Dobson gave me some more food to say sorry, but I didn't mind because I had got extra rations that day. I knew from now on, that when my bowls were put on the floor, I would have to move pretty sharpish and eat my food, before Katy came round trying to share it.

Mrs Dobson seemed to have more energy these days and had bought a baby harness so she could put Katy into it and take me for walks at the same time. These were happier times, and I gradually began to get fitter and slimmer with these extra exercises. Once again, I was able to walk through the wood and onto the heath and run around and sniff things to my heart's content.

Little did I know what was lying in store for me in the weeks ahead.

CHAPTER 2.

A few weeks passed in what I would call a normal existence and I was often taken for walks with Larry and Mrs Lawson joining us on some days. Then came a period where I was lucky to even get out of the house.

I heard Mrs Dobson telling Mr Dobson that there was a virus going round that made us dogs unwell. Apparently, the vets had recommended that dogs should be kept under strict control and not allowed to wander around. Also, they should avoid meeting up with other dogs.

It was a really miserable time for me as I was mainly confined to the house and only allowed out to play in the garden when the weather was fine. Unfortunately, it seemed to rain a lot during this period, and I spent a lot of time peering out of the window hoping the rain would stop.

I think Mrs Dobson realised I still needed my exercise and occasionally she would strap Katy into her harness and carry her on her back whilst she took me for a walk round the houses. Even then I had to walk on a lead, when really, I would have preferred to just roam around on my own.

Still, I was grateful just to be out and about in the fresh air and occasionally I saw Larry on my walks. Sometimes I would see him in his garden with his nose pressed up against the gate and I woofed to say 'hello' to him. Once or twice, we met Mrs Lawson walking Larry in the street. On these occasions Larry and Mrs Lawson would have to use the pavement on the other side of the road whilst we used the other.

The two ladies used to stop and have a conversation across the road, and Larry and I waved to one another. It was a very strange situation, but apparently it was for our own good.

Eventually, things started to improve, and I was now able to go for longer walks, but I had to avoid other dogs who had a bad cough, just in case I caught the virus.

Then one morning, Mrs Lawson called at our house with Larry and enquired if we were going walking that day. It was a fine sunny day and Mrs Dobson thought it was a good idea, but it would take a little while before she had got Katy ready for the outdoors.

Mrs Lawson said she didn't mind waiting and was supplied with coffee and biscuits whilst Mrs Dobson got Katy ready. Larry and I had a good chinwag, catching up with the local news.

"Did you get this bad cough that has being going around, Larry?" I asked.

"No, not me," replied Larry, "but Charlie the Collie who lives in the next street, he caught it and I think he was quite poorly for a while."

I said, "I think he must be feeling better, because I saw him walking with his owner yesterday, but he did seem to have lost a bit of weight. You know the way he liked his food and didn't take enough exercise."

"Gosh, yes," said Larry, "you would have thought a Collie would be quite sprightly, but poor old Charlie was not one for charging around was he."

Mrs Dobson had got Katy ready by now and she was strapped into her harness and Mrs Lawson helped Mrs Dobson put Katy on her back.

"It's a lovely day for a walk. Shall we go onto the heath today, Vera?" asked Mrs Dobson.

"Good idea, Eliza," replied Mrs Lawson. "Oh, by the way, that reminds me. Do you remember old Mr Barnard that lives in the big house up near the heath?"

"No, I can't say that I do," replied Mrs Dobson.

"Yes, you do," said Mrs Lawson. "You must remember him. That was the house where Larry and Saffy caught that robber with the gun."

"Oh, yes. I remember now," replied Mrs Dobson. "Has something happened to him?"

"Well, my friend Rita who works in the Post Office, seems to know everything that goes on in this town. She told me that Mr Barnard has had to go into a Care Home and his house has been sold," said Mrs Lawson.

"Oh, I wonder who will be moving in?" said Mrs Dobson.

"Well, Rita says she has heard that some wealthy Russian chap and his wife have bought it," said Mrs Lawson, "but whether she is right or not, we will have to wait and see."

Larry and I exchanged glances as we heard this news. We both liked Mr Barnard and he was extremely grateful when we caught the robber and bought a load of treats for us as a reward. We hadn't seen anything of him for a while, so perhaps he was not feeling quite so well.

Once everyone was ready, we started out on our walk. The first part took us through the woods, and Larry and I were let off our leads and allowed to run free. We soon had our noses to the ground sniffing out who had been this way recently.

Larry took one side of the path, and I took the other and after a while we changed sides. Then Larry barked to say he had found a new smell, so I went to join him. It was quite a faint smell, so it was not recent.

Larry thought it might be a bear, but I had never heard of bears in our woods and suggested it might be old Brock the badger or one of Freddy the fox's relations. After a few yards, we lost the smell completely.

We carried on with our walk and reached the heath. We wondered whether we should turn left or right when we got to the heath, but the two ladies and Katy were a little way behind us, busy talking.

"Come on Saffy, let's go and look at Mr Barnards house," said Larry.

"Good idea," I replied. "I'll just make sure the ladies see which way we go."

As soon as I saw that Mrs Dobson had noticed where we were going, Larry and I trotted off along the path that ran around the edge of the heath. There were some high hedges separating some of the big houses from the heath, but when we reached Mr Barnards house, there was just a small hedge that marked the boundary.

It looked as though Freddy the fox and his friends had made a hole in the bottom of the hedge, and Larry and I were able to squeeze through and stand on the lawn of Mr Barnards house.

There was a big lorry at the side of the house and men were taking things from the house and loading them into the lorry. They seemed to be very busy and sometimes two or three of them had to help carry a big item of furniture out of the house and take it to the lorry.

The two ladies and Katy arrived soon afterwards, and Mrs Dobson exclaimed, "Oh, it looks as though you were right, Vera. It seems as though Mr Barnard is moving out today."

"Yes, it looks as though they have almost finished. I wonder if the new people will move in today," said Mrs Lawson.

Larry and I looked at one another and I said, "I hope the new people have got a dog, Larry."

"Well, if they have, I hope it is a nice dog and not too posh for the likes of us. Do you know any Russian dogs, Saffy?" asked Larry.

"No, and I don't speak any Russian, do you?" I replied.

"No, I don't," admitted Larry, "but I'm sure we would get along just fine."

Shortly afterwards, the two ladies called us back to them and we continued our walk along the heath.

Three days later, Mrs Dobson took me for a walk again. We walked through the wood and out onto the heath, where I decided I would take another look at Mr Barnards house.

Mrs Dobson didn't seem to object, so I ran on ahead and squeezed through the hole at the bottom of the hedge. I came to a stop and stared with amazement.

There standing on the lawn looking at me, was a cream coloured cockapoo just like me, but with a little pink ribbon fixed to her collar.

We stood looking at one another for a few seconds and then with a bark she ran across the lawn to join me.

I woofed, "Hello. My name is Saffy, what are you called?" I was half afraid that she would not understand me, especially if she was Russian.

"I am called Princess," she replied. "We moved here from London, yesterday."

"Are you Russian?" I asked.

"No," she laughed. "I was born in this country, but I believe my owners Mr and Mrs Gromikov are from Russia originally. I often hear them talking about Russia, but it must be a long way away. Is that your owner calling you?"

"Yes. That's Mrs Dobson and we live on the other side of the wood. I hope we can meet each other again," I replied.

"Yes, if ever you are passing this way, call in and see me," said Princess.

"Sometimes I am with my friend Larry the Labrador. I'm sure he would love to meet you as well," I replied.

"As long as he is not a rough dog," said Princess. "I'm afraid I don't like rough dogs. I'm just not used to them."

I replied, "He is not rough, but sometimes he gets a bit playful and oversteps the mark. Don't worry, I'm sure you will like him, Princess. He's quite a handsome dog in some ways. Look, I'd better go because Mrs Dobson is calling me again. I hope to see you soon, bye."

I ran back through the hedge to where Mrs Dobson was waiting.

"It looks as though you have been meeting one of the new residents, Saffy. I hope you made a good impression," said Mrs Dobson.

I woofed to say that I hoped I had as well, and Mrs Dobson just smiled and Katy on her back just blew some bubbles.

CHAPTER 3.

I was just dying to see Larry and tell him about meeting the new dog at the big house near the heath, but several days passed without meeting up.

Then one morning, Mrs Dobson strapped Katy into her buggy, put my lead on and then heaved a big parcel onto the back of Katy's buggy.

"Come on Saffy. I've got to take this big duvet to the dry cleaners and the walk will do you good," she said.

Now this was very interesting. I had heard Mr and Mrs Dobson talking about duvets before and I think it is like a big blanket thing they put on their bed, but what interested me more was this business about dry cleaning.

I hate having baths, so if there was something that got me clean in the dry, then I was very interested to find out what was involved. It seemed as though you had to go to a special shop if you wanted to get dry cleaned.

We walked into town, but Mrs Dobson had to keep stopping as the big duvet balanced on the back of the buggy, kept slipping and she had to readjust the load.

Eventually we arrived at a shop and Mrs Dobson exclaimed, "Here we are Saffy. This is the dry cleaners. Thank goodness we have arrived. That duvet was really awkward. I don't think I'll be doing that again in a hurry. I'll use the car next time."

She managed to get the door open and squeezed in with the buggy and the duvet, whilst I just managed to creep in before the door swung shut. Now let's have a look at this dry cleaner.

There were lots of big machines making a noise as the clothes inside them could be seen going round and round. I looked hard but couldn't see anywhere that I could stand and be dry cleaned. In addition, there was a funny smell to the place. It was not a smell I had come across before. A sort of chemically smell and not one that I was particularly keen on.

I watched as the lady on the other side of the counter put Mrs Dobson's duvet into a big machine and then she pressed some buttons which made the machine start up and I could see the duvet inside the machine going round and round.

"Come on Saffy. The duvet is being dry cleaned and I'll pick it up later," said Mrs Dobson.

I was mighty glad to get out of that shop quick. If that was dry cleaning, there was no way I wanted to be put into a big machine and sent spinning round and round. No, I would stick to my baths as usual and just put up with it.

Mrs Dobson pushed the buggy home and I just trotted along beside it, but when we reached our road, Mrs Dobson walked up the path to the Lawson house and rang the bell.

I could hear Larry barking inside and shortly afterwards Mrs Lawson opened the door and invited us all in.

"Hello, Eliza. Got time for a coffee and a chat?" enquired Mrs Lawson.

"Yes please, Vera. We've just taken our duvet down to the dry cleaners and I'm just about done in," replied Mrs Dobson.

I went to talk to Larry and whilst we stayed out of the way of the humans, we kept within earshot as we liked to listen to what they were saying on occasions.

Mrs Dobson was saying that the new people who had moved into the big house up near the heath had a dog just like me, but she hadn't seen anyone else up there.

Larry said, "Have you met this new dog, Saffy?"

"Yes," I replied. "She is just like me, perhaps a bit younger and she wears a pink ribbon on her collar."

"Does she speak Russian?" asked Larry eagerly.

"No. She was born in this country and her name is Princess," I replied.

"Is she good looking?" asked Larry very intrigued.

"Yes, I suppose so. I've told her about you," I replied.

"What did she say? Would I be able to meet her?" asked Larry getting very excited.

"I think you would be all right, as long as you are not too rough. She doesn't like rough dogs, so you would have to be on your best behaviour and not get too excited," I replied.

"Oh, I can't wait to meet her," declared Larry with his tail wagging vigorously.

But Larry was to be disappointed as it was several days later before he called round to see us, with Mrs Lawson in tow.

It was another bright sunny day, but not too warm and once Katy was ready, strapped in her harness on Mrs Dobson's back, we all set out for the woods.

Larry could hardly contain himself today. He charged off straight through the woods, hardly bothering to sniff the smells on either side of the footpath. He kept urging me to 'hurry up' as he was so eager to reach the heath.

When we reached the heath, we had to wait for the ladies to appear in view before we struck off along the heath towards the big house.

"Just slow down a bit, Larry," I said. "Just remember, Princess does not like rough dogs, and you are so excited at the moment, she might think you are a bit too boisterous."

"Oh, yes," said Larry guiltily. "I'll just try and control myself a bit better."

It was no good. Larry was still charging on ahead of me towards the big house, but when he got to the hedge by the big house, he suddenly stopped and said, "Hey Saffy. Come and have a look. Someone has dropped a load of treats on the ground. M'm, that was delicious," he said gulping down a treat.

I ran up to where he was standing and sure enough, it looked as though a whole bag of treats had been dropped on the ground.

I started to sniff them warily, because it is not often you find a whole load of treats dropped on the ground, but they seemed to be the real thing and Larry was gulping them down quick like there was no tomorrow. He didn't seem to be suffering from any detrimental effects, so I stepped forward and picked one up to eat it.

Just as I put the treat into my mouth there was a quick whooshing noise, and I was yanked off my feet. I saw out of the corner of my eye, that Larry had also been yanked off his feet and we were now suspended in the air, caught up in some sort of net.

We had walked into a trap.

The net was closing in tighter around us and both Larry and I were jumbled up together. His face was pressed in close to my body and one of his legs had jammed its way into my mouth and I was unable to bark.

I saw a stockily built man wearing a funny hat on his head, emerge from the bushes and whilst we were struggling to get free, but just making things worse for ourselves, the man put Larry and I into a large sack and closed the top.

As the last bit of daylight disappeared, I realised that we had been 'DOGNAPPED.'

Mrs Dobson and Mrs Lawson were deep in conversation as they walked along the edge of the heath.

"I wonder if we will see anything of the new people in the big house today," said Mrs Lawson.

"We might be lucky, Vera, but the other day, we only saw their dog," replied Mrs Dobson. "Have you heard any more about them?"

"Only what my friend Rita has told me," replied Mrs Lawson. "Apparently their name is Gromikov and he is a rich Russian who has made his money in the Petro-Chemical industry. His wife is a bit younger than him and there is a suggestion that she was once a model."

Ahead of them on the heath footpath, they saw a strange squat built man emerge from the bushes, with a large sack he was carrying over his shoulder. He was walking away from them and had a small pork pie type of hat on his head.

The two women took no notice of him and very soon approached the low hedge that was the boundary of the big house where the Gromikovs lived. They expected to see their two dogs on the lawn on the other side of the hedge, but of Saffy and Larry, there was no sign.

"Where have those dogs got to now?" declared Mrs Lawson. "I hope they are not making a nuisance of themselves up at the house."

"You know what they're like, Vera. Always seeking new adventures," said Mrs Dobson. "Perhaps we had better start calling them."

The two ladies began calling for Larry and Saffy to return, but it was to no avail. Larry and Saffy had disappeared.

Meanwhile, the man with the pork pie hat was steadily stomping his way along the footpath at the side of the heath until he reached a road.

There was a small green van parked at the end of the road and the man with the pork pie hat made straight for it. He opened the back door of the van and inside was a metal cage. He opened the door of the cage and placed the sack inside.

Having done so, he secured the door of the cage, shut the back door of the van and climbed into the driver's seat. He sat there for a few minutes munching on a chocolate bar and then with a satisfied grin on his face, he drove off away from the heath.

CHAPTER 4.

Mrs Dobson and Mrs Lawson were quite surprised that Saffy and Larry had run off like that and not answering their calls.

"Perhaps they've scented an animal or something and have gone to investigate," suggested Mrs Lawson. "You know what they're like for following trails."

"You might be right Vera, but even then, Saffy usually comes back when I call," replied Mrs Dobson.

The two ladies continued to call for Saffy and Larry, but there was no response and now both women were starting to get cross.

"That's it. Larry's overstepped the mark this time. It will be quite a while before I bring him up here again," said Mrs Lawson huffily.

"Yes, and Saffy will have to be taught a lesson that she has to come back to me when I call," added Mrs Dobson.

The two of them continued to call for Larry and Saffy, but still there was no sign of the dogs.

Gradually, the feeling of crossness began to be replaced by one of worry and this was reflected in their voices when they called.

"Hang on a minute, Eliza," said Mrs Lawson. "Let's think about this rationally. You've got Katy to look after as well. We expected to find the dogs on the lawn of the big house, but they are not there. I'll go and shout for them further up the heath and if I find them, I'll ring you on your mobile. Why don't you go round by the road and call at the big house and see if the dogs are there?"

"That's a good idea, Vera," replied Mrs Dobson. "If they are there, I'll ring you."

As Mrs Dobson went to move off, something crunched underneath her foot. It was a doggy treat.

"Oh look, Vera. Someone has dropped some dog treats. It's a wonder we didn't find the dogs here scoffing the lot," said

Mrs Dobson. "Anyway, I'd better get going as it is quite a long walk to get to the big house by road."

As Mrs Dobson walked back through the wood, she occasionally heard Mrs Lawson calling for the dogs out on the heath.

The man with the pork pie hat was now driving his little green van through the centre of town and was being held up by some slow moving traffic.

In the back of the van, Saffy and Larry were still entangled in the net inside the big sack, but Larry had managed to get his leg out of Saffy's mouth, and they were trying to find a comfortable position for the rest of their journey.

They were both getting quite hot inside the big sack and Saffy suggested they stop struggling as it was only making things worse.

Faint sounds reached the two dogs of vehicle engines, and they ventured their opinions on whether they had heard a bus or a lorry. At one point they came to a stop, and they heard a beeping noise. Both dogs agreed it was the noise made by a pedestrian crossing when pedestrians had the green light to cross the road.

The van began to move again and gradually the sounds of other traffic faded away. There was just the hum of the tyres on the road surface, but after a while this changed as the van left the road and drove up a gravel lane. Once or twice the two dogs were thrown about in the back as the van negotiated some potholes, but soon afterwards the van came to a stop and the engine was switched off.

Mrs Dobson had made her way through the wood and was now walking up the drive of the big house. It was a rather grand property with a turning circle at the front for cars.

Undeterred, Mrs Dobson made straight for the front door and rang the bell. There was a barking noise from inside and just for a moment, Mrs Dobson fancied she had heard Saffy, but then she remembered the Gromikovs also had a cockapoo.

After a long wait, the door was eventually opened by a tall slim woman with dark long hair. She was expensively dressed in designer clothes and had a large gold bracelet on her wrist.

"Can I help you?" she enquired with just a trace of a foreign accent.

"I'm sorry to bother you," began Mrs Dobson, "but we've lost our dogs up on the heath and wondered if by any chance they might be on your property."

"Why would they want to come here?" asked the woman.

"My dog is a cockapoo called Saffy," said Mrs Dobson, "and the other day, she met your dog which is also a cockapoo I believe."

"I don't remember my Princess meeting any other dogs," said the woman.

"Your hedge that abuts onto the heath has a small hole at the bottom, probably made by the foxes. Anyway, Saffy found the hole and met your dog on your lawn the other day," replied Mrs Dobson.

"Oh," replied the woman. "I'll get my husband to sort that out. We don't want our Princess to go wandering off."

At that moment, Katy who had been quietly listening to the conversation in her harness on Mrs Dobson's back, decided she wanted to join in as well and let out a wail.

"Oh, you've got a baby on your back," exclaimed the woman. "Look, I would invite you in, but we are still unpacking and there are boxes everywhere. I haven't seen your dogs or heard them. What are their names and what are their breeds?"

"My dog is Saffy, and she is a cream coloured cockapoo, just like your dog. Larry is a black Labrador, and he belongs to my friend Vera Lawson. I'm Eliza Dobson and we live over in The Timbers."

"Nice to meet you Eliza," said the woman shaking her hand. "I'm Irina. Irina Gromikov. Why don't you give me your telephone number and I can call you if your dogs turn up here. Just step inside a moment whilst I find a pen and paper."

Mrs Dobson and Katy stepped inside the front door and were immediately accosted by a cream coloured cockapoo with a pink ribbon on her collar.

"You must be Princess," said Mrs Dobson allowing the dog to sniff her hand. "You haven't seen anything of my Saffy today, have you?"

Princess did not reply, but just rolled over for her tummy to be tickled.

A few minutes later, after she had given Irina Gromikov her telephone number, Mrs Dobson was walking back down the drive, occasionally calling for Saffy, only to be met with silence and no dog.

She decided to give Vera a ring and when the call was answered, it seemed that there was still no sign of either dog.

"Look, you go on home with Katy," said Mrs Lawson. I'll hang around up here on the heath for a while calling them and asking folks if they have seen them. You never know, they might have made their own way home and are waiting for us to turn up."

"Yes, all right, Vera. I'll go home and let you know if they are there or not," said Mrs Dobson making tracks for The Timbers.

When the van stopped, Larry and Saffy inside the sack kept very still and quiet. The listened hard as the man got out of the van. They heard his feet on the gravel and then they heard a man's voice say, "How did you get on, Ormerod?"

"Piece of cake, Willie. I told you she would be unable to resist a few treats. The only problem is, I had to scoop up her friend, a black Labrador as well," replied Ormerod.

"Ah well, it can't be helped. You'd better put them both in the same pen. The main thing is you've got the dog," said Willie.

The two dogs heard the sound of feet on the gravel again, and then the back of the van was opened up and they heard the door of the cage being undone.

Suddenly they were yanked off their feet as Ormerod picked up the sack and swung it over his shoulder as he marched away from the van.

Mrs Dobson arrived back at The Timbers half expecting to see two dogs waiting for her. Whilst she wished they would be there just to solve the problem; her hopes were to be dashed.

She rang Mrs Lawson to inform her of the situation, and Mrs Lawson said she would stay on the heath a bit longer and would call in to see Mrs Dobson on her way home.

Ormerod stomped his way across a back yard to where there was a row of metal cages. At present all the cages were empty, but in each cage was a small wooden hut which provided some shelter from the elements.

Ormerod opened one of the cages, stepped inside and opened up the sack.

Saffy and Larry lay tangled together in the net, blinking at the sudden exposure to daylight.

Ormerod unceremoniously tipped them out of the sack onto the floor of the cage and then began to disentangle the dogs. As he did so, he backed away towards the open door of the cage and as the dogs became free of the net, he quickly stepped outside and shut the door, securing it with a bolt.

He made his way back to a farmhouse and said, "that's it, Willie. Both dogs are caged up and I'll give them some food and water later. I think it's time you started making up the note."

"Yeah, okay. Don't panic. It's almost ready and when it's done, you can take it into town and post it in a letterbox. I hope you bought the stamps I asked you to the other day," said Willie.

"Uh, no. Sorry, I forgot, Willie," replied Ormerod.

"You big numbskull. Have I got to do everything round here," grumbled Willie.

"Sorry Willie. I'll call in at the post office first," said Ormerod.

41

"Yes, you do that Ormerod. And don't forget to stick a stamp on the envelope before you post it. Can I trust you to do that, or should I hold your hand just to make sure? I don't know what our mother made of you, I really don't," said Willie heading for his study.

CHAPTER 5.

Saffy and Larry, once they had disentangled themselves from the net, stood, shook themselves and then stretched their bodies after being confined in the big sack.

They watched as Ormerod made his way across the yard towards a house, half hoping he would come back and open the gate of the cage they were in.

"What's going on, Saffy?" asked Larry

"I don't know, Larry, other than the fact we appear to have been dognapped," replied Saffy.

" Oh dear," said Larry. "I don't like the sound of that."

"Neither do I," said Saffy. "I wonder why they captured us?"

"Perhaps it's because you are quite famous Saffy," suggested Larry. "Everyone in town seems to know who you are."

"I think it must be more than that," replied Saffy. "Anyway, it looks as though we may be here for some time, so we ought to make ourselves comfortable. I hope it doesn't rain because there is no roof to this cage."

"If it does, we can shelter in that hut thing in the corner," said Larry. "That is, if you don't mind sharing with me."

"Yes, all right, but I hope they bring us some food and water soon. My tummy's beginning to rumble. I didn't get the chance to eat any of the treats up on the heath, unlike you," declared Saffy.

Mrs Lawson had now returned from the heath and had given up any hope of finding the dogs. She was now sitting in Mrs Dobson's kitchen nursing a cup of coffee and a biscuit.

"It's no good, Eliza," she said. "I called and called and called, but those dogs never answered. I don't believe they are on the heath. I asked someone walking by and they hadn't seen any dogs today."

"Oh dear, what are we going to do?" exclaimed Mrs Dobson.

"Well, I know one thing's for sure, Lionel will not be going down the Jolly Drover tonight. Not until he has been up to the heath calling for the dogs," declared Mrs Lawson.

"I just don't understand it," said Mrs Dobson. "They are usually so well behaved. It's not like them at all. I can't think what has happened to them. It's almost as if they have been spirited away."

"Yes, well you might be quite near the mark there, Eliza," said Mrs Lawson. "I was having a think about the situation when I was calling the dogs up on the heath. Do you remember seeing that funny chap walking away from us with a big sack on his back?"

"Oh yes. He had a funny sort of hat on his head," said Mrs Dobson. "You don't think he had anything to do with their disappearance, do you?"

"I don't know," replied Mrs Lawson, "but you remember those treats lying on the ground. My Larry would not have been able to resist those, and I am just wondering if they have been trapped and taken away."

"Oh no," cried Mrs Dobson. "Not my Saffy. Do you think we should call the Police?"

"I think it might be a bit early for that," replied Mrs Lawson. "Shall we wait until the morning to see if they have turned up. If they haven't, then we ought to ring the Police."

"Yes, that's a good idea, Vera. I'll send my Hubert up on the heath as well, after he has had his dinner, once he comes home from work," said Mrs Dobson.

"Perhaps they could both go up there together," said Mrs Lawson. "I'll send Lionel round to see you this evening."

Back at an isolated farm just outside of town, Willie was just completing his note, with Ormerod lounging in an easy chair scoffing yet another chocolate bar.

Willie carefully put the note into an envelope which he laboriously, but carefully addressed.

"Right, you lazy git. Here is the note," said Willie handing the envelope to Ormerod. "Can I trust you to buy a first class stamp, stick it on the envelope and then post the envelope in the post box?"

"Yeah, sure, Willie," replied Ormerod. "Uh, I don't suppose you've got any money to buy the stamp, have you? I seem to have spent my money this week."

"Ye Gods!" exploded Willie. "Have you spent all your money on those chocolate bars. You'll make yourself ill you will. If you keep stuffing your face, you'll go off bang one day."

"I don't want to go off bang," declared Ormerod worriedly. "I promise, I'll buy a stamp and not a chocolate bar."

"Well make sure you do," said Willie handing over some money. "Now be off with you, or you will miss the last post."

Ormerod took the money and shuffled out of the house. A few minutes later, the little green van was heading down the lane back into town.

In The Timbers, Mrs Dobson was rather worried. She kept going to the window and looking out. Then she went to the door and opened it, half hoping that Saffy would be sat on the doorstep, waiting to be let in.

At the Lawson house, Mrs Lawson was also looking out of the window and opening the door, but there was still no sign of Larry or Saffy.

It was starting to get dark when Ormerod returned to the farmhouse in the little green van. He walked triumphantly into the kitchen where Willie was drinking a cup of tea.

"I did exactly what you told me to," he said to Willie. "I remembered to stick the stamp on the envelope before I posted it."

"Well done, Ormerod," said Willie. "As a reward, you can now go and give our guests some food and water. You know where everything is, so you should be able to get that right."

Ormerod happily trotted off to an outhouse and soon the sound of metal dishes could be heard as he prepared some food for Saffy and Larry. He carried the two dishes across to the cage and left them outside the door, whilst he went and filled two bowls with drinking water. Then he opened the door of the cage and stepped in, bringing the food and water with him.

He put the dishes on the ground, closely watched by Saffy and Larry who had retreated to the back of the cage as they were uncertain about this rather rotund individual before them.

"Here we are Princess. There's some nice doggy food for you. I apologise if it isn't up to your usual standard, but we can't afford to buy top price food," laughed Ormerod.

Saffy seemed a bit perplexed by this, but Larry only had eyes for the two dishes of food and was trying to work out, which one held the biggest amount.

"Sleep well little Princess," said Ormerod backing out of the cage and securing the door. "I'll see you in the morning and bring your breakfast. It's only a first class service here, provided by yours truly. You'll find your bedding in the hut, so sleep tight."

The two dogs watched him disappear across the yard and then Larry said, "Why did he keep calling you Princess, Saffy?"

"I'm not really sure, Larry. I rather think he is under the impression he has dognapped the new dog called Princess but has taken me instead."

"Perhaps they will let us go when they realise they have made a mistake," said Larry.

"Oh, I do hope so," replied Saffy. "Now which bowl is yours? I must admit I am feeling rather hungry."

That evening, Lionel Lawson called at the Dobson house and spoke to Hubert Dobson.

"Have you had your dinner, Hubert?" he enquired.

"Yes thanks, Lionel. Are you ready for the heath? I take it Larry has not returned home," said Mr Dobson.

"No not a sign of him. I was going to suggest that when we get to the heath, you go one way and I'll go the other. That way we will cover more ground. I hope you've got a good torch as it will be rather dark up there," said Mr Lawson.

An hour later, both men returned home having been unsuccessful in their search for the missing dogs.

As the evening wore on, it began to get rather chilly and both dogs retired to the hut. As Ormerod had promised, there was some bedding on the floor of the hut and both Larry and Saffy made themselves at home.

To start with they talked quietly to one another about their predicament and then as it got late, they snuggled up together to keep warm and gradually drifted off to sleep.

Larry seemed to go to sleep quite quickly and from time to time he gave a quiet snore, but Saffy had trouble sleeping. All the events of the day kept chasing each other around her brain and it was sometime later before she eventually drifted off to sleep.

CHAPTER 6.

The next morning dawned bright and sunny and before he went to work, Mr Dobson was up on the heath calling for Saffy and Larry. Apart from an early morning dog walker walking their collie dog, he didn't see a soul.

Feeling rather dispirited, Mr Dobson finished his breakfast and went off to work.

Whilst Mr Dobson was on the heath calling for the dogs, the two dogs in question were just stirring from their sleep inside the hut at the isolated farmhouse.

Saffy was the first to emerge from the hut and stretched herself to get the kinks out of her body and Larry joined her a few moments later.

"Good morning, Saffy. Did you have a good night's sleep?" asked Larry.

"Not really," replied Saffy. "I kept thinking about what has happened to us, but when I did drop off to sleep, I had a really strange dream."

"Really. What was your dream about?" asked Larry eagerly.

"This is the strange bit, Larry. I was rowing a boat across some water at night, and I had Katy sat in the back of the boat. The only thing was, Katy was a bit older than she is now and she could talk. The water was ever so calm and there was a moon shining that night. I asked Katy if she would like to touch the moon and she said that would be lovely, so I got her in the boat and rowed out onto the water. As the water was so calm, the moon was reflecting in the water and when we were in the right position, I told Katy to put her hand in the water and touch the moon. When she did it, she was ever so thrilled."

"Gosh, that is a strange dream Saffy," exclaimed Larry. "I didn't know you could row a boat."

"I can't," said Saffy, "that's the strange thing about it."

"What do you think it all means?" asked Larry.

"I'm not sure," replied Saffy. "All I can think is that I miss my home and the Dobsons and that I was dreaming about being with them again."

"Do you think we will ever see our homes again?" asked Larry.

"I do hope so," replied Saffy. "We've got to believe we will see the Dobsons and Lawsons again someday."

"What do you think we should do?" asked Larry.

"There's not much we can do at the moment. I hope that man brings us some more food and water soon, because I think it is time for our breakfasts. All we can do is just watch to see what happens and if we get the chance, we will have to try and escape," said Saffy.

"Good thinking, Saffy," declared Larry. "I wonder if they will take us for a walk today, because I do like my exercise."

At The Timbers, Mrs Lawson had called round to see Mrs Dobson.

"I take it your Saffy has not come home yet, Eliza," enquired Mrs Lawson.

"No. There's still no sign of her at present. Hubert was up on the heath before he went to work, but she didn't answer his call," replied Mrs Dobson

"I think it is time we called the Police," said Mrs Lawson.

"Yes, I think you are right, Vera, but what will we say to them? I mean are we reporting two dogs which have strayed or are we saying they have been stolen?" said Mrs Dobson.

"Good point, Eliza," said Mrs Lawson. "Why not say the two dogs are missing, which is most unlike them, and we think they may have been stolen by a man with a funny hat."

"Yes, that sounds better. I'll ring them right away," said Mrs Dobson picking up the telephone.

In the farmhouse, Willie Wilkins had dragged himself out of bed and gone downstairs to make some tea. He looked out of the window and saw the two dogs were in the cage, looking expectantly at the house.

Muttering under his breath, Willie stomped back upstairs and banged lustily on Ormerod's bedroom door.

"Come on you dozy git, Ormerod. Time to get up and go and feed our guests. Always remember, they are our investment for the future, so go and take good care of them," ordered Willie dragging the bedclothes off the bed.

"What did you do that for?" spluttered Ormerod who had been deep in slumber.

"You spend half your day asleep and the other half eating chocolate bars. Get yourself up and go and feed the dogs," demanded Willie slamming the door behind him as he left the room.

Ormerod got himself up and dressed. He quite liked dogs, so this was one chore that he didn't mind carrying out. Willie was always ordering him about and sometimes it all got rather confusing for him, and he didn't do things right. Still, feeding the dogs was simple enough and he set off with a happy heart.

Just after ten o'clock that morning, P.C. Griffin pulled up outside the Dobson house in his car. He made his way up the path and was about to ring the doorbell when Mrs Dobson quickly opened the door.

"Have you found them? Have you found Saffy and Larry?" she asked breathlessly.

"Good morning, Mrs Dobson. I'm afraid I haven't. I'm only just responding to your telephone call," said P.C. Griffin.

"Oh, in that case, you'd better come in," said Mrs Dobson crestfallen. "Vera, that's Mrs Lawson is here as well if you want to speak to her."

"Yes, I most certainly do," said P.C. Griffin. "This really is most unlike Saffy, I must say. Every time I have met her, she seems very obedient and not the sort to run away. You don't think she has gone off on one of her adventures again, but this time has got lost, do you?"

"We did think about that," replied Mrs Dobson, "but we really think this time it is more serious. We think the dogs have been taken by someone else."

"What makes you say that?" asked P.C. Griffin.

"You tell him, Vera. I don't think I could bring myself to talk about it," said Mrs Dobson.

So, Mrs Lawson told P.C. Griffin about finding the dog treats on the ground, right by the hedge where the Gromikovs lived, and also about the strange man who had a funny pork pie type hat on his head, who was walking away from the area with a large sack slung over his shoulder.

"The Gromikovs? I don't think I know them," said P.C. Griffin.

"They've just moved into Mr Barnards house up by the heath," said Mrs Dobson.

"Oh yes. I had heard he was going into a Care Home," said P.C. Griffin. "Also, that description of the man with a pork pie hat on his head seems to ring a bell. I can't pin it down at the moment, but I expect it will come to me in due course. I'd better get back to the Police Station and circulate the descriptions of your dogs, but if they turn up in the meantime, can you please let us know."

As P.C. Griffin drove away, Mrs Dobson said, "Well, I don't suppose there is anything else we can do now, just wait. Do you fancy another coffee, Vera?"

Ormerod had refilled the empty dishes with dog food and water and placed them on the ground just by the cage gate. He carefully undid the bolt securing the gate and said, "Here we are Princess. It's time for your breakfast. I don't know the name of your friend, but he seems a nice dog."

Larry woofed to tell him his name, but both dogs had retreated to the back of the cage allowing Ormerod to open the cage door and step in with the dishes.

Once he was in, he put the dishes on the ground and Larry rushed forward to eat his food. As he did so, Ormerod laughed and stroked him on top of his head before calling out,

"Come on Princess. You'd better get your food before your friend scoffs the lot."

Saffy barked, "Stop calling me Princess. My name is Saffy."

Ormerod just laughed again and stepped back out of the cage, securing the door with the bolt again. He stood for a short while, watching as the two dogs ate their food, and then he ambled back to the farmhouse to find some food of his own.

It was almost lunchtime when the postman trudged up the drive of the Gromikov house and stuck some mail through the letterbox. Irina Gromikov was still busy unpacking boxes, and it was another hour before she noticed the mail had been delivered.

Two envelopes were for her husband, but the third envelope had been addressed to "The Occupants". The envelope had been hand written in bold capital letters. Curiosity got the better of her, so she opened the envelope.

Inside was a single sheet of paper with words cut out of newspapers and magazines stuck to it. It was a message, but one which clearly mystified her. It read, "We have your Princess. If you want to see her again, put ten thousand pounds in a carrier bag and leave it by the bench in the park as shown on the map, at 9 o'clock Friday morning." There was a childish drawing of a map, and the bench was indicated by a red 'X'.

With a cry of alarm, Irina went in search of Princess who she had not seen for at least half an hour but found her curled up in an empty box in the dining room. Gratefully, she picked Princess up and carried her to her husband's study where she knocked on the door before going in.

"Vladimir, this letter has just arrived in the post," she said handing over the letter and the envelope. "What does it mean?"

Her husband quickly read the note and glanced at Princess in her arms, before declaring, "It looks like a ransom demand, Irina. The only problem appears to be they have got the wrong dog," he added with a chuckle. "There is no way I am going to pay that sort of money without any evidence. I'll ring the Police just to let them know what has happened."

At the Police Station, P.C. Griffin was quite concerned. He had met Saffy many times and was quite fond of the little cockapoo. He also knew her friend that lolloping black Labrador, Larry, who always seemed so excitable. He didn't think that either dog would stray like that. There had to be more to it.

He had just finished circulating the description of the dogs and the man with the funny pork pie hat, when the phone rang. It was Mr Gromikov explaining he had received a ransom note which did not make sense.

Fifteen minutes later, P.C. Griffin was at the Gromikov house being shown the note, which he carefully placed into a clear exhibit bag and then put the envelope into another exhibit bag.

"I'll get these checked for fingerprints," he said. "This may tie in with a report we had of two dogs being taken up on the heath yesterday."

"Oh, you must mean Saffy and Larry," said Irina Gromikov. "I had their owner, Mrs Dobson here yesterday asking if I had seen them."

"I take it you hadn't seen the two dogs," asked P.C. Griffin.

"No, and after she had left, I went out and searched the grounds of the house just in case," replied Irina.

"I rather think the people responsible have taken the wrong dog," said P.C. Griffin. "I know Saffy quite well and I must say she looks very much like your dog Princess."

"Is there anything we can do?" asked Mr Gromikov.

"Well, for starters, I suggest you keep Princess safe for the time being and also if you get any more letters or phone calls asking for money, just let us know," said P.C. Griffin. "Did the envelope come with the rest of your mail, or was it delivered separately."

"I don't know," replied Irina. "I didn't hear the postman, but the envelope was between two other envelopes, so I assumed the postman delivered it."

"Right, thanks for letting us know about this. There are lots of enquiries to be made now, so I'd better be getting on with them," said P.C. Griffin taking his leave.

CHAPTER 7.

Saffy and Larry were getting quite bored being cooped up in their cage at the farmhouse. They kept looking towards the house, hoping the man with the funny hat would come and take them for a walk, but all they had seen of him, was when he walked around the premises doing other farm work.

"I don't think we will be getting much exercise today, Larry," commented Saffy. "We must try and keep our muscles in trim, so I suggest we walk around the cage several times."

"Good idea, Saffy. That man looks like he is too busy doing other jobs. Did you notice that funny thing he has stuck in his ear?" asked Larry.

"Do you mean an earring? You know like Mrs Dobson has in her ears," replied Saffy.

"No, I don't think it is an earring. It must be something else. Right shall we start walking, or do you want to go off on your own?" enquired Larry.

"No, we'll do it together. You go on the outside as your legs are longer than mine," replied Saffy.

P.C. Griffin had returned to the Police Station and handed over the exhibits of the letter and envelope to the Forensics Department, for fingerprinting. They promised him a reply within two days.

Next, he called on the C.I.D. and spoke to the Detectives. He explained about the report of the missing dogs and then the ransom note received by the Gromikovs.

The Detectives were very interested in the story and D.C. Webb was given the task of working with P.C. Griffin to try and solve the case.

"What are we going to do about the ransom money?" asked P.C. Griffin. "If there is no money left in the park on Friday morning, I hate to think what will happen to those two dogs."

"We've got two days to play with," said D.C. Webb. "Today is only Wednesday and perhaps we will be able to find the dogs in the meantime. If not, we might have to lay a trap and see who walks into it."

Saffy and Larry had been walking round their cage for some time and still no one had come to see them.

"Hang on a minute Larry," suggested Saffy. "I think we need to turn and walk round in the other direction. I'm getting quite giddy going this way."

"Okay," said Larry. "It's a pity they didn't give us a bigger cage. Oh, look out. Here comes that man again."

Ormerod was pushing an empty wheelbarrow across the yard apparently on his way to carry out another errand. When he saw the dogs watching him, he stopped and called out, "hello

Princess. I'll be getting your lunch ready for you soon, but Willie has given me all these jobs to do this morning. Sorry I can't stop any longer to talk to you."

With that, he was on his way pushing the empty wheelbarrow round the corner of a barn.

"What do you make of him, Saffy?" asked Larry. "I quite like him because he seems so friendly."

"He might be friendly, Larry, but don't forget, he was the one who captured us in the first place and has kept us locked up ever since," replied Saffy. "Just be ready to make an escape if the opportunity arises."

P.C. Griffin and D.C. Webb had been busy and eventually their enquiries led them to the Royal Mail Sorting Office on the outskirts of town.

They quickly ascertained that the Postman they needed to speak to was Joshua Crabtree. Unfortunately, Crabtree was still out on his rounds, but was expected back shortly. Whilst they were waiting, they were supplied with a cup of tea.

It was another fifteen minutes before Joshua Crabtree returned to the Sorting Office with his empty mailbag over his shoulder. He threw the bag onto a pile of other empty bags and sat down on a chair and massaged the backs of his calves.

"Cor, the old pins are playing up a bit today," he declared. "Is there any of that tea going, I'm fair parched."

Crabtree was supplied with his tea and introduced to Griffin and Webb.

"I wonder if you can help us Mr Crabtree?" began Webb. "I believe you were delivering to the big houses that border onto the heath, today."

"Yes, that's right," agreed Crabtree. "I wouldn't mind, but some of them have got awfully long drives and it doesn't make my job any easier."

"Did you deliver any mail to Mr and Mrs Gromikov today?" asked P.C. Griffin.

"Is that those Russians who moved into old Mr Barnards place?" asked Crabtree.

"That's the ones," said P.C. Griffin.

"Yes, I did now you come to mention it," replied Crabtree. "I think it was just three letters, that's all."

"I don't suppose you remember anything about the letters, do you?" asked D.C. Webb.

"Actually, I do," replied Crabtree. "I was sorting out the letters as I walked up their drive, and out of idle curiosity I suppose I did glance at the letters. There were two for him with London postmarks and the other was handwritten addressed to 'The Occupants'. It had a local postmark and I thought someone in the town was quick of the mark in writing to them."

"Good man," said D.C. Webb. "You've been very helpful in a case of dog stealing. We might need to take your fingerprints for elimination purposes later, but if we do, we will be in touch again."

Back at The Timbers, Mrs Lawson and Mrs Dobson were having a discussion about what else they could do to find the missing dogs.

"I think we might have to get some posters prepared saying the two dogs were missing. We could include photographs of the two dogs as well," said Mrs Lawson. "Then we could go round pinning them up in appropriate places where people might see them."

"That's a good idea, Vera," said Mrs Dobson. "I'll speak to Hubert about it when he comes home tonight. Meanwhile, I'll have to search to see if I've got any photographs of the dogs."

It was getting late in the day when P.C. Griffin called at the Post Office in the centre of town. D.C. Webb had been called back to the Police Station to deal with something else, so now he was making enquiries on his own.

There were two women clerks behind the counter, and they were dealing with a last minute rush of customers who needed their mail sent today.

P.C. Griffin waited until the queues had died down and then walked up to one of the women he knew by the name of Rita.

"Hello, Rita. I wonder if you could help me solve a crime," asked P.C. Griffin.

"I'll just close my counter," said Rita. "I'm sure Mabel can deal with any last minute customers."

A minute later, P.C. Griffin had Rita to himself.

"We're investigating a case of dog stealing, Rita. It seems that the persons responsible have demanded a ransom," said P.C. Griffin.

"Oh! How exciting," exclaimed Rita, "but how can I help you?"

"There are some new people in town, some Russians by the name of Gromikov," began P.C. Griffin.

"That's right, they moved into old Mr Barnard's house, up by the heath," said Rita.

"Yes, I thought you might know that Rita," observed P.C. Griffin. "Anyway, the ransom note was delivered to them, but I hasten to add, it is not their dog that has been stolen. It is a cockapoo called Saffy that has been stolen, along with a black Labrador called Larry."

"Not Larry," cried out Rita. "He belongs to my friend Vera Lawson."

"That's right," said P.C. Griffin.

"What do you want to know?" asked Rita determinedly.

"Well, it's a bit of long shot really, but have you seen any letters being posted to the Gromikovs yesterday?" asked P.C. Griffin.

"I didn't see one posted, but I did sell a stamp to a chap who had an envelope addressed to the Gromikovs," said Rita.

"Brilliant," declared P.C. Griifin.

"Yes, he seemed to be a slow, if you know what I mean. A bit thick, perhaps. He said he only needed one first class stamp and he had to stick it on this envelope. I saw the envelope and it was addressed to the Gromikovs. It was handwritten in block capitals. I thought it was strange at the time. How did this individual know the Gromikovs when they had only just moved into the area."

"Can you describe this chap?" asked P.C.Griffin.

"He was not that tall, but he was rather round, almost fat. The thing that struck me was he had a large head and perched on top was a funny little hat. I think they call them pork pie hats because they look like a pork pie," said Rita.

"Well done," said P.C. Griffin. "That ties in with the description we have of the person responsible. I don't suppose you know who he is, do you?"

"No, I've never seen him before, but from what people have said, he might be one of the brothers who lives on a farm on the outskirts of town. Apparently, their mother died and one of the boys was a bit simple," said Rita.

"I knew I did the right thing in coming to talk to you, Rita. You seem to know everything that happens in this town," said P.C. Griffin.

"I'll put my thinking cap on," said Rita, "and if I can remember the name of the people on that farm, or where it is, I'll let you know. I think I'd better give Vera a ring tonight when I get home. She must be out of her mind with worry."

That evening, Larry and Saffy were watching the farmhouse, waiting for the man to come and feed them. Eventually, he came ambling out of the house and made for one of the sheds and soon after deposited the dishes full of food outside the cage. He then went to fill the drinking bowls with water and put them on the ground near the cage door.

Saffy and Larry had backed away to the rear of the cage as the man unbolted the gate and stepped in with the dishes full of food and water.

"Here we are, Princess. Time for your evening meal," he laughed.

Larry rushed across the cage and attacked his dish of food, ignoring the man who was crouched near him. The man reached out and patted Larry on the head and chuckling, he backed out of the cage and bolted the door.

After he had gone, Saffy walked across to her dish and began eating her food. When she was done, both dogs laid out on the ground just in front of the hut.

"That might just be the last food we will eat here," said Saffy.

"What do you mean?" asked Larry concernedly. "Are they going to stop feeding us?"

"No. It's not that," said Saffy. "I've been watching that man carefully and he seems to be a creature of habit. If he does the same thing tomorrow when he brings our breakfast, we might be able to escape. This is what we'll do…"

CHAPTER 8.

By the time P.C. Griffin had returned to the Police Station, he was already an hour late in going off duty. D.C. Webb was now out, busy dealing with another matter, so there was no one he could confide in regarding the information that had come to light.

Under the circumstances, he decided the matter could wait until the next morning and he would tell D.C. Webb about it then.

Mr Dobson had arrived home and over dinner, his wife broached the subject of compiling some posters regarding the missing dogs.

"If they don't turn up soon, I think that is an excellent idea, Eliza," said Mr Dobson. "Have you got any photographs of the dogs?"

"Yes," said Mrs Dobson. "I found one that was taken last year, and it shows both Saffy and Larry playing together in the back garden."

"Well done, Eliza," said Mr Dobson. "I'll take it into work tomorrow and have a word with my boss. He might let me use the office equipment to make some posters up. How many do you think we will need?"

"As many as you can manage, dear," replied Mrs Dobson. "Rita and I will be putting them up all over town."

"If I buy the paper, there shouldn't be a problem," said Mr Dobson, "but I'll just need to speak to my boss first."

That night, Saffy and Larry were laid down inside the hut, peering out at the night sky. It was unseasonably warm that night, which was just as well, as neither dog was used to being exposed to the elements like this.

Larry soon drifted off to sleep and began softly snoring, but Saffy was unable to settle down, as thoughts kept running through her mind. It was sometime later before she eventually drifted off to sleep.

The sun was an early riser on Thursday morning and its rays shone straight into the hut where the two dogs were asleep. Larry was the first to awake and stepped outside to sample the early morning air and cock his leg in the corner they were using as a toilet.

Saffy continued to sleep for a while longer, but eventually the persistence of the sun's rays won the battle, and she was forced to rise and shine herself.

"I wish that man would hurry up and bring our food," complained Larry.

"I think it might be a bit early for him at present. Don't forget what I told you about trying to escape this morning. If we do, we might be home with our families by tonight," said Saffy. "I don't fancy sleeping in that hut another night."

P.C. Griffin started work at eight o'clock that Thursday morning and armed with a cup of tea, he made his way to the Criminal Investigations Department. D.C. Webb had also just arrived at work and was sat at his desk looking at some paperwork.

"How did you get on at the Post Office?" asked Webb as he saw P.C. Grifin enter the room.

"Very well, actually," said P.C. Griffin. "I think we struck gold."

He then proceeded to tell D.C. Webb about the information he had obtained from Rita. When he had finished, D.C. Webb leant back in his chair and said, "Any idea who these two brothers are?"

"Not at the moment," replied P.C. Griffin. "However, the description of the man with the pork pie hat rang a bell and I've been racking my brains overnight. I'm sure I have seen someone answering his description driving a little green van around town, but who he is, I'm none the wiser."

"Look, I've got to go to court this morning, so I'm likely to be out most of the day. See if you can draw up a list of farms on the outskirts of town," said D.C. Webb.

"Okay, and when I've done that, I will try and find out who lives there," said P.C. Griffin.

"Good man," said D.C. Webb, "but don't go charging in like a bull in a China shop. We may have to play this carefully as those two dogs might be in danger."

It was nearly nine o'clock before Willie Wilkins dragged Ormerod out of bed and gave him his orders to feed the dogs without delay.

Grumbling at being treated in this fashion, Ormerod set about filling the dog's bowls with food and water which he placed by the door of the cage. Saffy and Larry had moved to the rear of the cage as Ormerod opened the gate and stepped into the cage with the bowls of food and water.

He carefully set the bowls on the ground and then crouched down and rested on his haunches.

"How is my Princess today?" he asked. Receiving no reply, he continued, "You're going to make me rich tomorrow."

Saffy had been watching him carefully and when she thought it was the right moment, she barked to Larry, "Now, Larry."

With a woof, Larry rushed across the cage as if he was heading for his food, but at the last moment, he turned slightly and made for the man on his haunches.

The man watched him coming with slight concern, but then Larry jumped up with his front paws and licked the man on the face. The man let out a yell of delight and then a yell of concern as Larry's momentum pushed the man backwards and he landed on his bottom with his legs in the air, being straddled by a black Labrador dog.

As he fell backwards, his pork pie hat flew off his head and that strange thing in his ear fell out onto the ground.

Quick as a flash, Larry had spotted this strange thing from the ear and scooped it up in his mouth. He now ran triumphantly round the cage with this strange object in his mouth making funny whistling noises.

"Hey, that's my hearing aid you've got in your mouth. Bring it back here," yelled the man.

But Larry was having none of it and continued to run around the cage with whistling noises coming from his mouth.

The man was getting quite angry now and advanced into the cage threateningly. As he approached Larry, Saffy edged her way towards the door of the cage.

Larry watched the man approach and just before the man reached him, he tossed the hearing aid high into the air and it landed in the farthest corner of the cage.

The man was now totally confused and didn't know which way to turn first. In the end he made his way to pick up his hearing aid, but whilst he did so, Larry shot past him and made for the gate.

Saffy who had been watching things develop had already stepped outside the cage and as soon as Larry was free and out of the cage, the pair of them took to their heels and ran as fast as they could up the lane away from the farm.

Ormerod was now very angry and shouted at them to come back as he lumbered up the lane to try and catch them. There was no way he was likely to keep up with the two dogs, as fear leant them wings and they put a good distance between themselves and Ormerod.

Willie Wilkins had been enjoying his cup of coffee in the kitchen when he heard a rumpus outside. He got up and looked out of the window, in time to see Ormerod take off up the lane, shouting. Putting down his coffee, Willie went outside and called out to Ormerod, asking what all the shouting was about.

"It's those two dogs," spluttered Ormerod. "They jumped me and now they've escaped."

"You blithering idiot, Ormerod," shouted Willie. "I suppose you left the door open for them to escape. If you had half a brain, you'd be dangerous. Come on get the van out and we'll try and head them off before they reach the road."

Saffy and Larry had now slowed down their flight from the farm and were now trotting up the lane.

"Well done, Larry," puffed Saffy. "That was a good idea playing with that hearing aid thing. He completely forgot he'd left the door open."

"Yes, it was a good bit of fun, but I hope he doesn't catch up with us again, because he was very angry when we ran away," said Larry.

"We will just have to be careful not to get caught, won't we," replied Saffy sagely. "Hang on, Larry. That sounds like the van starting up at the farm. I think we had better get off this road quick before they come."

The two dogs quickly turned off the lane and into a ditch and from there they found a gap in the hedge which led to a field.

As they heard the sound of the van approaching, they lay down flat in some long grass and watched the van go past.

When the van reached the end of the lane, Willie stopped the vehicle.

"They can't have got this far yet," said Willie. "The devious little darlings must be hiding up. Right, you get out Ormerod and lay your trap with the net and some doggy treats and I'll go back to the farm and start looking for them down there."

"Okay, Willie," said Ormerod. "How long do I have to stay and wait for them, because I didn't have any breakfast this morning."

"You stay for as long as it takes," said Willie. "It's all your fault we are in this mess, and we were due to pick up the ransom money tomorrow. Perhaps we could still collect the money, even though we no longer have a dog to trade," he said wistfully.

"I just hope those dogs come along sooner rather than later," grumbled Ormerod getting out of the van with his net and doggy treats.

Saffy and Larry watched the van go past and then keeping close to the hedge, they trotted along the edge of the field towards the road.

As they neared the road, they heard the sound of voices and then the door of the van being slammed as Ormerod truculently got out. They watched as the van headed back to the farm and Saffy said, "We've got to be very careful now, Larry."

They peered through the long grass and watched as Ormerod, grumbling to himself, laid out a large net across the lane. Then they saw him open a bag of doggy treats and sprinkle them on the ground.

"Come on doggy, doggy," called Ormerod, "come and get your treats."

Saffy sensed that Larry was eager to get to the treats, but she laid a restraining paw on him and whispered, "No, Larry. Don't be tempted. That is how we were captured in the first place. Come on, lets follow the hedge in the field and hope it leads to town."

P.C. Griffin had taken all morning trying to locate all the farms on the edge of town by looking at a large scale map of the area, He now had a list of potential targets, but further enquiries were thwarted by the ringing of the telephone.

"Is that you, P.C. Griffin?" asked Mrs Dobson.

"Yes, it is. I was going to ring you this afternoon," said P.C. Griffin. "I was hoping I might have something positive to tell you."

"Is it true that Saffy and Larry are being held to ransom?" asked Mrs Dobson.

"We can't be sure that is the case. Mr Gromikov received a ransom letter from someone saying they had his Princess, but we know that is not true. We suspect they have got your Saffy by mistake and probably have got Larry as well," said P.C. Griffin.

"Do you know who these people are?" asked Mrs Dobson.

"We have several lines of enquiry," said P.C. Griffin vaguely, "but the ransom is due to be collected tomorrow morning and we hope to make an arrest and get your dogs back to you as soon as we can. If we have any further news, I will keep you informed, but at the moment, all we have is speculation."

"Yes. Please do that, P.C. Griffin. You don't know how worried both Vera and I are," said Mrs Dobson

CHAPTER 9.

Whilst Ormerod sat in the bushes guarding his trap at the end of the lane, Larry and Saffy had made their away along the hedge away from the direction of the farm.

After a while they spotted several rabbits playing in the long grass enjoying the warm sunshine. As they approached, the rabbits scattered in all directions, alarmed at the sudden appearance of two strange dogs.

"Please don't run away," called out Saffy. "We are lost and need your help."

One of the larger rabbits paused in his flight but kept close to his burrow as he turned to look at the new arrivals.

"What is the meaning of this?" he demanded. "Who do you think you are interrupting the young rabbits in their playtime?"

"We're awfully sorry," said Saffy. "We didn't mean to scare them like that. I'm Saffy and this is Larry, and we were captured by those men in the farm across the fields. We managed to escape, and we are trying to make our way back to town. Are we heading in the right direction?"

"Captured, were you?" said the rabbit. "Yes, I'm not surprised. You have to try and avoid those men at the farm. They are very dangerous and have caught several members of my family in their nets. They also have a gun which they shoot at us, but they are not very good and so far, none of us have been hit. Yes, if you keep going in this direction you will come to the town, but then you have to watch out trying to cross the roads."

"Oh, that's all right," said Saffy. "I know how to cross the roads, because I do my Green Cross Code to get safely across."

"I don't suppose you've got any food we could eat?" asked Larry. "You see, we had to miss breakfast in order to escape."

"There's loads of food all around you," laughed the rabbit, "that is if you like our vegetarian diet. Try a luscious blade of grass for a change."

"I'll pass on that for now," said Larry, "but if I get desperate later, perhaps I'll give it a go."

"It's time we got going, Larry," said Saffy. "Thank you for your assistance, your little rabbits can come out to play again."

The two dogs trotted off in the direction of town and when they reached the corner of the field, they looked back to see all the rabbits out having their playtime.

P.C. Griffin had been in touch with the local council and given them a list of the outlying farms. He requested details of the persons living there, but was told this might take a little while, but they would act on it as quickly as they could.

Feeling at a loss for anything else to do, he decided to walk around the town to see if he could spot the man in the pork pie hat, or his little green van.

He walked down the High Street without seeing the man or the van and then walked into the Post Office. He was fortunate to find it was a quiet period and he was able to talk to Rita behind her counter.

"Hello, Rita," said P.C. Griffin. "Have you had any more thoughts on our man with the funny hat?"

"I've been racking my brains on the matter," replied Rita. "It's so frustrating I can't remember his name. I have a feeling that it begins with a 'W'. It might be Williams or Wilson, something like that."

"Okay, Rita. I thought I would check in with you," said P.C. Griffin. "I know how you feel. I seem to recall seeing this chap driving a little green van around town, but I'm blowed if I can recall anything else about him."

"I spoke to Vera last night," said Rita. "She's quite upset about losing Larry and I believe that Mrs Dobson is very upset at losing Saffy. If I remember anything else, I'll ring you at the Police Station."

Meanwhile, Saffy and Larry were still making their way across the fields in the direction of town. They had slowed right down, now they were out of danger away from the farm.

"I do wish we could find some food, Saffy," complained Larry.

"Yes, I know," replied Saffy. "My tummy is beginning to rumble as well, but I think what we need most of all is water."

"There's a herd of cows in this new field," said Larry. "Perhaps they might know where we can get some water."

As they walked towards the herd of cows, most of them moved away, but one cow stood there eyeing them suspiciously.

"What are you two dogs up to?" she mooed.

"We're sorry to bother you," said Saffy, "but we are lost and trying to find our way back to town."

"Yes, and we are both hungry and thirsty," added Larry.

"If you keep going, you will come to the town," said the cow, "but I don't see what the problem is. There is plenty of grass here to eat."

"Oh, no! Not more grass again," moaned Larry.

"Is there any water nearby?" asked Saffy ignoring Larry's theatrics of lying on his back with his legs in the air, clasping his tummy with his front paws.

"Yes. There is a water trough in the corner of the field over there. There is always plenty of water in there," replied the cow.

"Thank you," said Saffy politely. "Come on Larry, stop rolling around acting the fool. We've got to get back to town."

"If you run all the way, you might just reach town before it gets dark," said the cow putting her head down to munch some more of that succulent grass.

The two dogs made their way to the corner of the field and sure enough, there was a metal trough. By standing on their hind legs and putting their paws on the top of the trough, both dogs were able to drink some water.

"Let's have a rest here for a while," suggested Saffy. "Then we can have another drink of water before we set off again."

"Good idea, Saffy," said Larry. "I think I've had enough exercise for one morning, but it sounds as though we still have a long way to go before we reach town, so we had better not stop for too long."

P.C. Griffin decided his next port of call would be the Gromikov house up by the heath. He was fortunate to find Mr Gromikov at home and was shown into his study.

Good afternoon, Constable," said Mr Gromikov. "Have you found those missing dogs yet?"

"No, not yet, sir," admitted P.C. Griffin. "I was just calling to see if you had any further correspondence from the people who stole the dogs."

"No. They have not been in touch since," said Mr Gromikov. "Do you really think they have taken this Saffy, instead of my Princess?" he asked.

"Yes. It seems the most likely suggestion," admitted P.C. Griffin. "We have got several enquiries in hand at the moment and are waiting for answers, but the ransom is due to be paid tomorrow morning and I don't know what we are going to do about it."

"I take it the dog owners can't afford to pay the ransom," enquired Mr Gromikov.

"No. I think it is beyond their means, much as they love their dogs," replied P.C. Griffin.

"Would it help if I paid the money on their behalf," asked Mr Gromikov.

"That's a very generous offer, sir, but we do not encourage people to pay ransom money if possible. However, I will mention it to the C.I.D. when I get back to the Police Station."

Saffy and Larry had set off after their rest and were now walking along following the hedges in the direction of town. The sun was starting to sink lower in the sky, but now in the distance they could see the beginning of the houses on the edge of town.

"Come on Larry don't dawdle. There's the town up ahead," said Saffy.

"I don't know if I can go much further," replied Larry. "I don't think I've had this much exercise in a long while and certainly not on an empty tummy."

"Come on, you can't give up now. We've got to find somewhere to shelter for the night because it will be getting dark soon," said Saffy.

"Yeah, yeah, all right, stop nagging me, Saffy," replied Larry. "Sorry, I'm just a bit ratty through being so hungry."

"Yes, I know," said Saffy. "I'm feeling that way too."

The two dogs continued to plod their way across the fields and then they came to a field where several sleek looking horses were grazing the grass. The horses ignored the two dogs but kept a wary watch on them out of the corner of their eyes.

Just as the daylight was beginning to fade, the two dogs came across some buildings. It looked at first glance to be a farm and Larry said, "Oh no, Saffy. We've gone round in a big circle, and we are back at the farm."

"No, I don't think so, Larry. This looks more like some stables where the horses are kept," replied Saffy.

Just then they heard the sound of voices and not wanting to be discovered just yet, the two dogs hid behind a pile of timber and watched.

They saw a man come out of the farmhouse and he whistled. He was joined almost immediately by a greyhound who literally bounded out of the house.

"I'm just going to check on the horses, Mavis," he called out. "Can you get the dog his food whilst I'm gone?"

Saffy and Larry watched as the man and dog made their way out of the farm towards the fields. Shortly afterwards, they saw a woman come out of the house carrying a bowls full of food and a bowl with some water. She put them down outside the door and disappeared back into the house.

Saffy and Larry sat watching for a short while and as the woman had not returned, Larry said, "I can't stand it any longer. The sight of that food is sending me mad."

"Okay, Larry, but be careful and don't go making any noise. Just remember, save some for me," said Saffy as the two dogs quickly and quietly made their way across to the farmhouse.

Saffy stopped to listen at the door, but it sounded as though the woman was busy in the kitchen, judging by the sounds coming from within. Larry on the other hand did not stop and was soon attacking the food in the bowl. He was quickly joined by Saffy who did not want to miss out on some food and in next to no time, the food dish was empty.

Then the two dogs turned their attention to the water bowl and that too was quickly emptied. Although their tummies were not quite full, both dogs felt a bit better, and they returned to the pile of timber just as the man and the dog returned from the fields.

Both Larry and Saffy felt a bit guilty at eating the greyhound's food, but their need was greater. They heard the man call out, "I thought I asked you to get the dog his dinner, Mavis."

"I did," came the reply from the kitchen. "It's right by the back door."

"Well, there's none in the bowl now. I bet it's that ruddy fox come sneaking in again. I think I'll have to keep my shotgun ready, just in case," said the man.

"Oh, stop your moaning," said the woman. "Hang on a minute, I'll get the dog some more food."

Shortly afterwards, the greyhound was tucking into his dinner and Saffy began to have thoughts about where they could sleep that night.

P.C. Griffin had now returned to the Police Station and was telling D.C. Webb about Mr Gromikovs offer to pay the ransom money.

"No, we can't allow that," said Webb. "What we could do is lay a trap by leaving a carrier bag full of newspapers by the bench in the park. We could watch and see if anyone comes to collect it and if they do, we can nab them."

"I've not had a reply from the council yet," said P.C. Griffin. "What do you want me to do?"

"I think tomorrow, you ought to come into work in your civilian clothes and you can take the carrier bag to the park. I'll be watching with my colleagues from C.I.D. So, all you've got to do is leave the bag and then just walk away," said Webb.

As the night became darker, Saffy and Larry stayed hidden behind the pile of lumber and once the lights in the house were switched off, Saffy stood up and stretched her legs.

"Come on Larry, there is an empty horse box over there. We could sleep in there tonight," said Saffy.

The two dogs made their way quietly to the empty horse box and their luck was in as there was straw on the floor.

Very soon, two very tired dogs were fast asleep on the warm straw.

CHAPTER 10.

At a quarter to seven on Friday morning, there was a stirring in the kitchen of the farmhouse, as Gilbert the greyhound woke from his sleep. He stepped out of his basket and stretched, getting all the kinks out of his muscles, and stood waiting for one of the humans to get up and let him out for his early morning constitutional walk around the farm.

It was quite a lazy life for a greyhound, but it had not always been like this. Sometimes he had to be up early and go for training runs and other days were spent travelling to different greyhound racing tracks. Oh, how he missed the roar of the crowds as he chased the mechanical hare around the track.

But those days were long gone and as he grew older, he was put out for retirement and sold to his current owners who took care of him.

Ten minutes later, someone got up and let him out into the yard. He stood outside the kitchen door smelling the air of a new day and then began his patrol of the premises.

In the Dobson household, Mr Dobson was getting ready for work and Mrs Dobson was just getting Katy up out of her cot.

"I wonder if we will hear any news about Saffy today?" pondered Mr Dobson.

"Oh, I do hope so," replied his wife. "I do hope Saffy is all right. I know it has only been a matter of a few days, but I do miss that little dog so much."

"Cheer up, love," said Mr Dobson. "My boss says if Saffy has not turned up by lunchtime, I can spend this afternoon printing the posters you wanted."

"That would be great," said Mrs Dobson. "At least I feel we will have done something useful at long last. Vera and I will go round town tomorrow pinning the posters up in prominent places."

"I think quite a lot of people know Saffy," said Mr Dobson, "But I don't suppose many of them know she is missing. Anyway, I'd better get going or I'll be late for work. Ring me if there is any news."

Gilbert had almost completed his patrol, when something unusual caught his eye. At first, he couldn't believe his eyes. Then he became quite indignant.

There in a horsebox, were two dogs fast asleep on the straw. One was a cream coloured dog and the other was a black Labrador.

"Oi, you two. What's your game?" he barked.

Both dogs had been in a deep sleep, but Saffy reacted the quickest, whilst Larry lazily yawned and stretched himself.

"We're sorry. We didn't mean to cause any bother," replied Saffy anxiously.

"Who are you and what do you mean by intruding onto the premises. I'm the only dog allowed on this farm," huffed Gilbert importantly.

"My name is Saffy and this is Larry," said Saffy by way of introduction. "We were captured by some bad men and taken to a farm, but we managed to escape yesterday and we are trying to get back to town to find our owners."

"Captured, were you?" said Gilbert. "Someone tried to capture me when I was in my prime for racing, but my owner saw what was happening and managed to stop them."

"We walked all day yesterday and we were so tired, we just couldn't walk any further. That's why we were sleeping in this horsebox," said Saffy.

"Yes, and we didn't have any food either," added Larry. "Well, not until we had yours."

"Yes, sorry about that," said Saffy, "but we were very hungry and tired, but we did see the lady put some more food down for you."

"Yes, well," huffed Gilbert. "I suppose there was no harm done, but the master thinks it was foxes that stole the food and now he's got his gun handy just in case."

"Oh, dear," replied Saffy.

"It's probably best if you make yourselves scarce as soon as possible. You don't want him to see you. There's no knowing what he will do," said Gilbert.

"Yes, that sounds like a good idea," said Saffy. "Come on Larry, don't be a lazy bones. I think it is time we made a move."

"I don't suppose there is any chance of some food and water?" asked Larry hopefully.

"No, they don't feed me for at least another hour, but if it's water you want, you'll find a water trough in the horse field. It's on your way when you go into town," said Gilbert.

"Thank you," said Saffy. "Come on Larry, time to move."

At the Police Station, P.C. Griffin wearing his civilian clothes of a sports jacket and jeans entered the C.I.D. office to find a scene of activity. A carrier bag was placed on D.C. Webb's desk and it was being filled with old newspapers.

"Here we are," said D.C. Webb. "Here is your ransom money."

P.C. Griffin looked at the carrier bag and could plainly see it was full of newspapers. "That won't do," he said. "Anyone can see it is only newspapers in there."

"Good point," said D.C. Webb. "How about we tied the handles of the bag together and then cello tape the top, so no one can see into it."

"Yeah, that should do it," agreed P.C. Griffin. "What time do you want me to leave the carrier bag at the park?"

"The ransom note said leave it at nine o'clock, so if you enter the park just before nine and leave the bag by the bench they wanted, that's all you have to do. Then you just walk away and don't look back," said D.C. Webb. "The rest of the C.I.D. will be all around the park waiting to pounce if anyone tries to claim the bag. I think it is time we all moved out and took up our positions."

Saffy and Larry had found the water trough in the horse field and had a good drink of water. They were watched by some curious horses who did not seem to object to two strange dogs drinking their water.

Very soon they came to a housing estate and had to keep an eye out for cars on the roads. There seemed to be a lot of children walking with their mothers and Saffy and Larry walked behind them. They all seemed to be going in the same direction and very soon they reached the local school.

The children all ran into the playground and the mothers stood around by the school gates talking. One of the mothers had a black 'Scottie' dog on a lead and Saffy went to him and asked if he knew the way to a road called The Timbers.

"Och, I don't think it is around here, lass," replied the Scottie. "It's probably on the other side of town. Your best bet is to make your way into the centre of town and then ask again."

"Oh, we're strangers around here," said Saffy. "Which way is the town centre?"

"If you follow this long road to the end and then turn left, that is the main road into town, but you need to watch out for all the cars and lorries," said Scottie.

"Thank you, we will," said Saffy as she nudged Larry away in the right direction.

At the Wilkins farmhouse, Willie had set his alarm clock to get up early. He made sure that Ormerod got up early as well as he didn't like to see his brother sleeping in whilst he was up and about.

Over breakfast in the kitchen, Willie was making sure that Ormerod understood what he had to do that morning.

"Right, Ormerod," said Willie. "Tell me what you have got to do this morning."

"I've got to drive you in the van to town this morning, when you tell me to," said Ormerod.

"Very good, Ormerod," said Willie, "But what happens next?"

"I've got to drive you to the road by the park and then stop," said Ormerod.

"Well done," said Willie, "and then what happens?"

"I wait with the van while you go into the park and get the money. Then you come back and I drive you home and we can count out the money," said Ormerod triumphantly.

"If you can remember all that, Ormerod, what can possibly go wrong," laughed Willie looking at the clock. "I think it is time we made a move."

Saffy and Larry were now trotting alongside a busy main road. Most of the traffic was heading in one direction and Saffy correctly assumed this would lead them to the centre of town.

Some of the time they were able to walk on the pavement and on other occasions they trotted along the grass verge, but the roads were getting quite busy with traffic.

Then they reached a very busy road, but needed to cross it.

"How are we going to get across, Saffy?" asked Larry.

"Ah, I know how," said Saffy looking up the road towards some traffic lights. "Come on, I'll show you how to do it."

The two dogs trotted up to the traffic lights and watched the cars go by. Then Saffy stood on her hind legs and put her front paw on a box at the traffic light pole. There was a button in the middle of the box, and she pressed it.

Nothing happened for a little while, but suddenly, all the cars and lorries stopped and there was a beeping noise.

"Come on Larry, that's our signal to say it is safe to cross," said Saffy stepping out into the road.

Larry needed no further encouragement and stepped off behind her, looking at all the drivers in amazement as he crossed the road.

When they reached the other side of the road and the traffic began to move again, Larry said, "How did you know what to do, Saffy?"

"Well, for a start, I heard P.C. Griffin tell the children at school about using the crossing and I've seen Mrs Dobson do it as well," replied Saffy. "Come on, let's get going again."

P.C. Griffin was waiting in the C.I.D. office until it was time for him to leave with the carrier bag. The office was empty and quiet as everyone had gone to watch the park, ready for someone to pick up the carrier bag.

Whilst he was waiting, a girl from the Forensic Department came in and said, "We've had the results of the fingerprint checks we made on the ransom letter and envelope, and we have got a hit."

"Really, that is good news. Anyone we know?" asked P.C. Gilbert.

"Yes, there are some prints belonging to one William Wilkins," replied the girl. "He was arrested for stealing from shops about three years ago. I thought you'd be interested."

P.C. Griffin was just deciding what to do with this result, when he was approached by a clerical assistant who said, "the council have just dropped in a list for you. Apparently, you wanted to know who lived in various farms outside of town."

"That's right," said P.C. Griffin eagerly scanning through the list. Halfway down, he came across the names of William and Ormerod Wilkins.

This couldn't wait. He needed to tell D.C. Webb at once. He got onto the radio to contact D.C. Webb and passed the information he had received.

"Good work," said D.C. Webb. "We might need to follow that up later on, but it is time for you to deliver the carrier bag to the park. You might need to get your skates on."

P.C. Griffin had a quick look at the clock, grabbed the carrier bag and made for the door in a hurry.

Ormerod was sedately driving the little green van into town, with his brother Willie sat beside him. Traffic was quite busy, but Willie had allowed for this when deciding what time they should leave.

Ormerod was humming a little tune to himself, but Willie was trying to keep a look out for unfriendly faces.

Five minutes later, they arrived in town and Ormerod drove up the road alongside the park.

"Pull over here, Ormerod. This will do nicely," said Willie glancing at his watch. "Right, I'm off to stretch my legs for a bit," he said getting out of the van.

D.C. Webb who was sat in an unmarked Police car just up the road, saw the little green van pull up and stop. He remembered P.C. Griffin telling him about a little green van, so he sent a message to the other watchers to say that a possible target had arrived and that one man was just getting out of the van.

As Saffy and Larry walked along the roads leading into town, there were more and more houses and the occasionally shop and petrol filling station.

Saffy was leading with Larry just plodding along behind her, not taking too much notice of his surroundings. Suddenly Saffy came to a stop and Larry who was not expecting this ran into the back of her.

"What did you stop like that for?" he grumbled.

"I've just realised where we are, Larry," said Saffy. "I know someone who can help us get home."

CHAPTER 11

Willie Wilkins left the van and made his way into the park. There were trees all around it and whilst it was not a small park, it was not over large either.

There were bench seats dotted all around the park and they were all unoccupied, apart from one bench at one end, where two women were sat chatting.

Willie took a quick look at the bench where the money was to be left, but there was no carrier bag to be seen. He looked at his watch and realised there were still two minutes to go before the nine o'clock deadline was reached.

He stopped and looked carefully around the area, looking for anyone who might be watching him, but apart from the two women sat on the bench talking, there was no one else around.

He decided he would take a little stroll around the park, whilst he waited for the money to be delivered. As he did so, he passed the two women on the bench who were still talking and taking no notice of him whatsoever.

He took another look at his watch and noticed it had just turned nine o'clock. Where was that money? He would give them a few minutes longer.

P.C. Griffin was late in leaving the Police Station with his carrier bag. Also, he had underestimated how long it would take him to reach the park. He set off walking briskly, but one look at his watch told him he would be late if he carried on like this.

In the end, he was forced into a run, whilst clutching the carrier bag to his chest. It was going to be a close run thing whether he made it to the park on time or not.

Willie Wilkins was starting to get worried. Still no carrier bag. Something had gone wrong and they wouldn't be getting any money at this rate.

He kept looking at his watch and was getting agitated when he noticed a man running up the road to the park, clutching a carrier bag.

At last, this looked promising.

He watched as the man slowed to a walk and entered the park. The man looked all round and then walked up to the nominated bench. He looked all round once more and then deposited the carrier bag by the side of the bench.

Having done this, the man turned and walked out of the park.

Willie watched him leave the park and waited for a minute or two, in case the man suddenly returned. Satisfied that this was not the case, Willie tried to walk as casually as possible in the direction of the carrier bag.

Saffy and Larry were sat on the pavement looking across the road at a large red brick building.

"You say there is someone in there who can help us to get home," said Larry. "Who is it?" he asked.

"Well, I hope I am right," said Saffy, "but we have both been here before, but last time we came in a car."

"I can't say that I remember coming here before," said Larry. "I don't even know where we are. It's not an area that I recognise. Are you sure you've got the right place?"

"Yes, pretty sure," replied Saffy. "There's only one way to find out. We'll have to go in and see for ourselves."

Saffy made sure they crossed the road safely and they trotted up a brick paved drive to the front of the building. There didn't seem to be anyone around, so they walked towards the glass doors at the front of the building.

As they stood in front of the glass doors, there was a whooshing noise and the two doors slid open.

"Come on Larry, they open automatically let's get in quick before they shut," said Saffy.

Both dogs crossed the threshold and found themselves in the entrance foyer of the building. They were confronted with another set of glass doors, but this time the doors refused to open. Meanwhile, the automatic doors had closed behind them and they were stuck between the two sets of doors.

They looked in through the doors, but there was no one to be seen.

"Oh great!" said Larry. "We're prisoners again. That's just what we need."

"I'm sure someone will come along soon, but at least we are in the warm and dry for now," said Saffy.

Willie Wilkins had been under observation from the moment he got out of the van. D.C. Webb had watched him enter the park and then the two female detectives sitting on the bench talking confirmed he had arrived.

Although they ignored Willie as he passed by them, they kept the rest of the team informed of Willie's movements around the park.

As Willie walked towards the carrier bag, the two women left their bench and slowly started to walk towards him.

Willie couldn't believe his luck. It looked as though his scheme had paid off. They were going to be rich, well for a little while perhaps. He made straight for the bench and only had eyes for the carrier bag. Had he looked round, he would have noticed that suddenly people had materialised from their hiding positions all around the park and they were all closing in on him.

With a cry of delight, Willie picked up the carrier bag, which was all sealed up at the top. He gave it a little squeeze and it certainly felt as though there was paper money inside. He turned to walk back out of the park and as he did so, he suddenly noticed all these people closing in on him. There was only one thing left for him to do. He took to his heels and ran.

Saffy and Larry had been trapped in the foyer of the building for some five minutes, but then Larry spotted someone moving around inside.

He leapt to his feet and began barking trying to attract their attention, but although Saffy joined in as well, the person took no notice of them and disappeared.

"I don't know," grumbled Larry, "I think we'll be stuck here forever and I'm starving hungry and could do with a drink."

"Yes, it was a little while since we had a drink out of that trough," admitted Saffy, "but I'm sure someone will come along soon."

As she said it, a woman in a navy blue overall was seen inside the building. Both dogs began barking again to attract her attention, but is seemed that she could not hear them.

"Let's try jumping at the door to make a noise," suggested Saffy, and the two dogs jumped up at the door making it bang.

The woman in the navy blue overall, stopped and turned round to see what was making the noise. Then she peered closely and came towards the door.

Suddenly her face lit up with delight and she pressed some buttons at the side of the door and the doors opened.

Both dogs rushed inside and ran to the woman who bent down to give them a hug.

"Well, Saffy and Larry, fancy seeing you, but look at the state of you. It looks as if you've been sleeping in a haystack," said Mrs Vardy. "Where is Mrs Dobson and Katy today?" she asked looking round.

"See I told you we had been here before," said Saffy triumphantly. "This is the home where Mrs Dobson's mother lives and this is Mrs Vardy who is in charge."

"Well done, Saffy," said Larry, "you're a right little clever clogs you are. Do you think we might get some food and a drink soon?"

There was only one thought in Willie Wilkin's mind and that was to run back to the van and drive away, but there was a man coming towards him who was trying to block his escape.

As Willie ran towards D.C. Webb, Webb called out, "stop where you are. I am a Police Officer and you are under arrest."

"Not likely," thought Willie and at the last moment, swerved to go round D.C. Webb.

Webb was clearly anticipating something of the kind, and moved in front of Willie, but Willie had momentum on his side and charging down the park like a rugby player clutching a carrier bag, he barged into Webb, sending him flying onto his backside.

Willie looked round and saw all these other people running towards him, so he put on a spurt of speed and shot out of the park.

"Where's the van?" he muttered to himself. "Ah, there it is parked up the street."

Willie hurtled up the road to the van, opened the passenger door, jumped in and shouted, "quick Ormerod, let's go. The Police are after us."

As he struggled to put his seat belt on, there was no reaction from the driver's side of the vehicle. Ormerod was gone.

Exasperated and trying what to decide what to do, Willie looked out of the window and saw Ormerod leaving a shop across the road, carrying his supply of chocolate bars.

"Hurry up, Ormerod," shouted Willie. "The Police are after us."

This galvanised Ormerod into action. Slow as he might be on occasions, this was not one of them and he rushed across the road and jumped into the van.

He had no sooner sat in his seat when the van was surrounded by Police Officers. D.C. Webb reached in and removed the keys from the ignition.

"You are both under arrest for stealing dogs and blackmail. Where are the dogs now?" he asked.

"I don't know," replied Ormerod. "They overpowered me and escaped."

"They overpowered you and escaped," said D.C. Webb in amazement. "Well, you will be taken to the Police Station for questioning, but meanwhile, other officers will be searching your farm trying to find them."

"Does that mean we can't keep the money?" asked Ormerod.

"What money?" said D.C. Webb.

"The money in the carrier bag," replied Ormerod.

"There's no money in there," said D.C. Webb reaching in and opening the carrier bag for them both to see.

"You big dimwit, Ormerod," shouted Willie. "If you hadn't gone shopping for more chocolate bars, we could have got away"

"I was hungry, wasn't I. You didn't give me much breakfast today," replied Ormerod truculently.

CHAPTER 12.

Willie and Ormerod had been taken to the Police Station and whilst they were being escorted to the cells, D.C. Webb and P.C. Griffin were in a car speeding towards the Wilkins farm.

"Did you believe him when he said the dogs overpowered him and escaped?" asked P.C. Griffin.

"No. I think it was just a fairy tale," replied D.C. Webb with a laugh.

"I assume you looked in the back of the van, in case they had the dogs in there," said P.C. Griffin.

"Yes, as soon as the van had been brought to the Police Station, I unlocked the back and checked for myself. There were no dogs in there, but they had the back fitted out with a cage, just right to put stolen dogs in," replied D.C. Webb.

"I do hope we find those dogs at the farm," said P.C. Griffin. "I've quite taken a shine to little Saffy. She's a lovely intelligent dog and all the schoolchildren love her."

Ten minutes later, the Police car arrived at the farm. The two officers got out and looked around. The place looked deserted and no one answered the door when they knocked at the farmhouse.

"Did you find out who lives here?" asked D.C. Webb.

"Just those two brothers that have been arrested," replied P.C. Griffin.

"Ah well. We may as well start looking round," replied D.C. Webb.

It wasn't long before they found the cage with the door hanging open, where the dogs had been imprisoned. There were even two dishes containing dog food and two dishes containing water inside the cage, but of dogs, there was no sign.

"This looks like the place where they kept the dogs," said D.C. Webb.

"Looking at this, I rather think the dogs did escape," said P.C. Griffin, "but whether they overpowered him in doing so, I wouldn't like to say."

"Well, there's no sign of them now," said D.C. Webb. "I think we had better go back and talk to our prisoners."

Mrs Lawson had called round to see Mrs Dobson and the ladies were sat in the lounge with their coffee, watching Katy playing on the carpet.

"I take it you've not heard anything, Eliza?" asked Mrs Lawson.

"No, nothing at all," replied Mrs Dobson. "Hubert will be printing the posters this afternoon, then you and I can go around town tomorrow pinning them up. The worst part, Vera, is not knowing what has happened to the dogs."

"Yes, I know what you mean, Eliza, but at least you've got Katy to look after and keep your mind off it. I've only got Lionel, and when he has gone to work, I've got no one, so it's a lot worse for me," declared Mrs Lawson.

Further conversation was interrupted by the ringing of the telephone on a small table in the corner of the room. Mrs Dobson rushed across the room with a face full of excitement and anticipation and answered the phone.

As she spoke to the person on the other end of the phone, Mrs Lawson watched as Mrs Dobson's face turned to one of despondency.

"Oh, it's you, Mrs Vardy," said Mrs Dobson. "I hope mother is all right?"

"Yes, yes. She's fine," replied Mrs Vardy.

"Oh, I'm glad about that," said Mrs Dobson. "I don't think I could cope with mother being unwell, not at this moment in time. What can I do for you, Mrs Vardy?"

"Well, I was wondering if by chance you might have lost something?" said Mrs Vardy.

Mrs Dobson quickly thought about her handbag and purse and slowly said, "No, I don't think I have lost anything, Mrs Vardy."

"How about a couple of dogs?" asked Mrs Vardy with a chuckle.

"Saffy. You've got my Saffy, have you?" asked Mrs Dobson with excitement lighting up her face once more.

"Yes, and her friend Larry as well," replied Mrs Vardy. "They just walked into the home about ten minutes ago. They looked in a bit of state, as if they have been sleeping rough, but I've given them some water just to keep them going. Have you not missed them?"

"Missed them? Of course we've missed them Mrs Vardy. Someone stole them on Monday and we've been looking for them ever since. Oh, this is wonderful news. Can you keep hold of them until Vera and I can get to you? You've made our day for us," said Mrs Dobson putting down the phone.

"Did you hear that, Vera?" asked Mrs Dobson. "Saffy and Larry just walked into the home where mother lives. Mrs Vardy doesn't know where they've been, but it looks as though they have been sleeping rough."

"That's right on the other side of town," declared Mrs Lawson. "How on earth did they get right over there?"

"I don't know, but if you give me a hand getting Katy ready, we'll go over and get them straight away. Now who is that ringing?" wondered Mrs Dobson as the phone rang again.

She answered the phone and P.C. Griffin said, "I just thought I would update you on the search for Saffy and Larry, Mrs Dobson. We arrested two men this morning for stealing your dogs, but when we searched their farm, it looks as though the dogs have escaped."

"I know," said Mrs Dobson. "I've just had a phone call to say the two dogs have just walked into the Care Home where my mother lives on the other side of town. We're just on our way to go and get them."

"Oh, that is good news, Mrs Dobson. I knew that Saffy was an intelligent little dog. Can you let me know once you have confirmed it is them and have got them back, as I'll need to cancel all the circulations that have been put out," said P.C. Griffin.

"Yes, I most certainly will do that and I'd better let my husband know, because he was due to prepare some posters about the dogs this afternoon," said Mrs Dobson.

Willie and Ormerod were questioned by the Police about stealing the dogs. Willie said as little as possible, but could not explain how his fingerprints were found on the envelope and note sent to Mr Gromikov.

Ormerod on the other hand could not stop talking and described in great detail how he had caught the dogs in his net, because Willie had said they could get a lot of money for Princess. He refused to believe that he had captured the wrong dog and maintained he had looked after the two dog's welfare at all times.

When Willie was told they had captured the wrong dog, he commented, "Trust Ormerod to muck it up. I should've done it myself."

Katy was strapped in her car seat and Mrs Dobson drove her and Mrs Lawson across town to the Care Home.

"I've really missed not having Larry around," said Mrs Lawson. "I know he gets quite excitable at times and makes a nuisance of himself, but it's just a case of having him around the house."

"I know what you mean, Vera," said Mrs Dobson stopping at a red traffic light. "I keep thinking it is a nice day, let's take the dogs for a walk and then I realise the dogs are not there. I can't wait to see them again. Hubert was quite thrilled when I rang him at work. I think he will try and get home early tonight."

Five minutes later, the two women were walking into the Care Home, with Mrs Dobson carrying Katy in her arms.

As soon as they walked into the Home, they were swamped as two very excited dogs rushed to meet them and jumped up to say 'hello'.

Both Women crouched down and hugged their dogs, whilst the dogs responded by licking their faces. Even Katy was licked by Saffy, which made her giggle.

The two women thanked Mrs Vardy for looking after Saffy and Larry and Mrs Dobson went to pay a quick visit to her mother.

Whilst all this was going on, Saffy and Larry were impatient to go home.

"How much longer are they going to be?" moaned Larry. "Don't they know were starving hungry?"

"No, I think they are so happy to have us back again, they've not even thought about feeding us," said Saffy.

"Perhaps if we lie on our backs with our legs in the air and then put our front paws on our tummy, they might get the message?" asked Larry.

"We could give it a go," said Saffy.

The sight of both dogs on their backs with their paws on their tummies, was just too much for Mrs Lawson, who burst out laughing.

"Okay, you two. I get the message. We won't be much longer and then we will take you home for food. I'll just go and find Eliza."

CHAPTER 13.

It wasn't long before the two dogs were taken back home to The Timbers. Mrs Dobson parked on her driveway and everyone got out.

As Larry and Mrs Lawson prepared to go to their own home, Larry said, "well, that was quite an adventure, Saffy. I know you've had lots of adventures in the past and I was glad that I was part of this one."

"It's not an adventure that I would want to repeat," said Saffy. "In fact, I wish it had never happened. It will take a little while to get over it and my paws feel as if they have walked for miles."

"Well, yes. When you put it like that," said Larry, "I have to agree with you. I didn't like having to stay in that cage, but it was more of an adventure when we made our way back into town, all by ourselves."

"I expect I will see you in a day or two, Larry," said Saffy. "I can't wait to get indoors, have some food and then curl up and rest in my favourite basket."

Mrs Lawson took Larry home and as Saffy had anticipated, she was given some food and went to sleep in her basket. However, Mrs Dobson kept coming into the room, just to make sure that Saffy was still there and had not disappeared again.

That evening, Mr Dobson arrived home from work a little earlier than usual and made a big fuss of Saffy. Then Mrs Dobson declared that Saffy looked like a ragamuffin and needed a good brushing.

As Mrs Dobson began to brush Saffy, she noticed how thin the little dog had become during the few days she had been away from home.

"I rather think those people that took Saffy, didn't feed her properly." she said to Mr Dobson

"Either that, or Saffy lost weight through all that walking," replied her husband. "I expect her paws might need attention as well," he added.

Apart from being let out into the back garden, there was no walking for Saffy for the next two days, as she recovered from her ordeal.

The following Monday, Mrs Lawson called round with Larry.

"How are things, Eliza?" asked Mrs Lawson.

"I think we are just about back to normal, Vera," replied Mrs Dobson.

"Well, I think Larry is desperate for a walk and I was going to take him up onto the heath. We wondered if you would like to join us," asked Mrs Lawson.

"Good idea," replied Mrs Dobson. "I think it will be safe enough now those two men have been arrested."

Ten minutes later, everyone was ready and set off walking through the woods. Saffy and Larry led the way, putting their noses to the ground as they sniffed the familiar smells.

Then Larry said, "Shall we go and see if Princess is in her garden, Saffy?"

"Okay," replied Saffy. "I don't think there will be anyone trying to capture us today."

Five minutes later, the two dogs approached the hole in the hedge that led to Princess's house. The only difference was, the hole was no longer there. Mr Gromikov had fenced over the hole with wire mesh, to stop Princess escaping onto the heath.

Larry who was desperate to meet Princess, stuck his nose through the mesh and barked, "I can't see her at the moment."

Suddenly, there was a yelp from the other side of the hedge and Princess appeared on the other side of the mesh. Larry stepped back, embarrassed and Saffy took his place.

"Hello Saffy," said Princess. "I hear you have had a big adventure. Is this your friend Larry?"

"Yes, and he is very keen to meet you," replied Saffy.

Further conversation was curtailed as Mrs Gromikov appeared and called Princess away, but just at that moment, Mrs Dobson and Mrs Lawson arrived.

An animated conversation took place between all the ladies and Mrs Gromikov invited them all round for coffee.

As they all walked back round by the road to reach the house, Larry said, "Why did you tell Princess that I was keen to meet her? You made me feel all embarrassed."

"Well, it's true," said Saffy, "You are keen to meet her. Just remember, don't get too excited, because she does not like rough dogs."

As the ladies were taking their coffee, the dogs were left to fend for themselves. Larry after being a bit bashful decided to show off and try a few tricks that he knew.

Saffy and Princess watched him amusedly, and Princess said, "You are so lucky to have such a handsome friend. I hope you will all come and see me again."

The following weekend, as the weather was fine, Mr Dobson declared he was taking everyone for a day out. Katy was strapped in her special car seat and Saffy was strapped in alongside her as Mr and Mrs Dobson drove off to another town.

Mr Dobson stopped the car in a street which was lined with trees on both sides and everyone got out. They walked through the trees and came to a big lake where there were some boats.

Mr Dobson paid a man some money and then said, "Come on, I'm going to take you all out for a trip on the water."

Mrs Dobson and Katy sat at the blunt end of the boat and Saffy was allowed to sit next to them. Mr Dobson sat on a seat in the middle of the boat and then began to row them steadily out into the middle of the lake.

Everyone was enjoying themselves and then Saffy remembered her dream. Whilst there was no moonlight as the sun was shining brightly, the only other difference was that it was Mr Dobson doing the rowing and not Saffy.

"Perhaps that was what my dream was all about," mused Saffy as she enjoyed a little sleep in the warm sunshine, rocked by the movements of the boat.

THE END

ACKNOWLEDGEMENTS.

Thanks once again to June for her painstaking proofreading and suggestions for improving the text. Also to John Snowden of Snowden Photography for his work on the book cover.

ABOUT THE AUTHOR.

Keith Fleming was born on the Isle of Wight and attended Carisbrooke Grammar School. He is a former Police Officer and Criminal Justice Casefile Manager with a degree in Laws.

He is married with one daughter, two step daughters and four grandchildren. He is now retired and enjoys gardening, playing bowls and writing novels. He now lives in Dorset.

Printed in Great Britain
by Amazon